PENGUIN
COMES HOME

Based on text by Louise O. Young
Illustrated by Larry Elmore

AMAZING ANIMAL ADVENTURES

For my three chicks: Hannah, Henry and Charlie — L.O.Y.

I would like to dedicate this book to my parents, Norman and Marie Elmore. When the cold winds blew in my life, they were always there for me, providing a warm, safe place to learn and grow. Thanks. — L.E.

Book design: Marcin D. Pilchowski
Book layout: Jennifer Kinon
Editor: Laura Gates Galvin
Editorial assistance: Brian E. Giblin

First Edition 2004
10 9 8 7 6 5 4 3 2 1
Printed in China

Acknowledgements:
   Our very special thanks to Rob Nawojchik of the Mystic Marinelife Aquarium for his review and guidance.

Library of Congress Cataloging-in-Publication Data

Young, Louise, 1951-
      Penguin comes home / by Louise O. Young ; illustrated by Larry Elmore.--1st ed.
         p. cm. -- (Amazing animal adventures)
      Summary: A penguin searches under the ice of Antarctica for food for herself and her growing chick, while avoiding being eaten by seals. Includes a fact page about penguins.
      ISBN 1-59249-324-6 (hardcover) -- ISBN 1-59249-325-4 (micro pbk.)
      ISBN 1-59249-326-2 (pbk.)
      1. Emperor penguin--Juvenile fiction. [1. Emperor penguin--Fiction. 2. Penguins--Fiction. 3. Antarctica--Fiction.] I. Elmore, Larry, ill. II. Title. III. Series.

PZ10.3.Y868Pe 2004
[E]--dc22
                                                                                            2004002582

PENGUIN
COMES HOME

Based on text by Louise O. Young
Illustrated by Larry Elmore

Soundprints
Where Children Discover...

An icy-cold wind blows across Antarctica. The wind hits icebergs, which break free to float on the water.

Although it is springtime, the weather is bitter cold.

As the sun rises, an emperor penguin swims far below the water's surface. She has been down deep for 20 minutes, searching for food to feed her hungry chick.

Penguin sees a school of silverfish. Stretching her neck, she pinches one fish in her beak and gulps it down. She looks for more, but they have darted away. Her lungs need air. She swims to the surface.

Penguin sees more yummy food, but she can't stop to eat. She needs to breathe. She bursts from the water with her wings open. Then she settles back in the water, breathing the cold air.

Penguin dives back under to
find the food she missed. She snatches
krill with her beak. As Penguin hunts, she
turns back toward the sea ice where her
chick is waiting.

Suddenly, other penguins leap and dive into the water. Penguin is startled. She slips under the waves, shooting toward the sea ice.

Penguin sees squid. Yum! She grabs and eats her tasty meal.

Penguin senses a shape nearby. She rolls over to look, ready to race for safety. The shadow moves closer. It is a small seal. Penguin swims away fast.

Another dark shadow appears. This time it is a very big seal! In a panic, Penguin races toward the sea ice. Snapping his jaws, the seal chases after her. He closes in. Penguin reaches the edge of the ice.

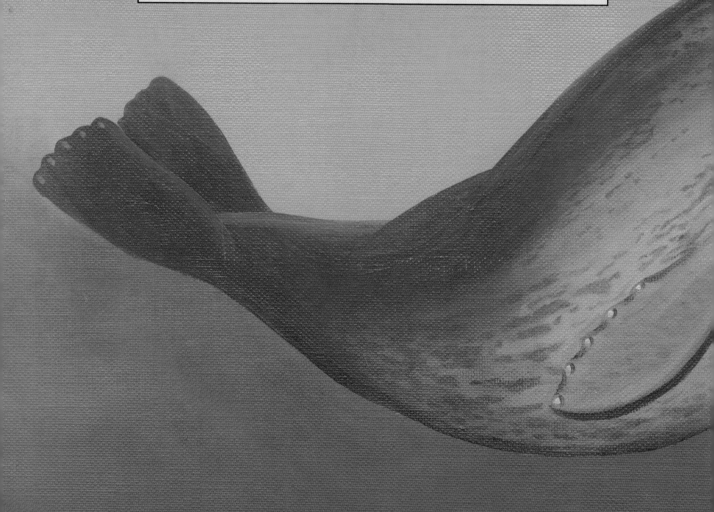

Penguin thrusts herself out of the water, flying into the air and onto the ice. She digs her toes into the ice and pushes away from the edge, sliding to safety.

The seal sinks back into the water and disappears. Penguin is safe. Now she must check on her chick!

Penguin shuffles away from the water and marches on.

Soon she joins more penguins. For hours they walk and slide through the wind.

As Penguin nears home, she calls with a trumpeting sound. The other penguins join in. In the distance are groups of chicks.

Penguin sings for her chick. All the chicks whistle and call. She pushes through them, listening for her chick. There he is! His dark eyes shine in his white face. His body quivers as Penguin moves closer.

Penguin opens her mouth and her chick reaches in and gobbles up the food Penguin brought him.

Weeks later, most of the sea ice has melted. Penguin's chick is ready to swim. He wiggles and bumps against the other chicks until he is finally at the edge of the ice. He waits a moment and then pushes off, into the cold water that becomes his home.

THE EMPEROR PENGUIN LIVES IN ANTARCTICA

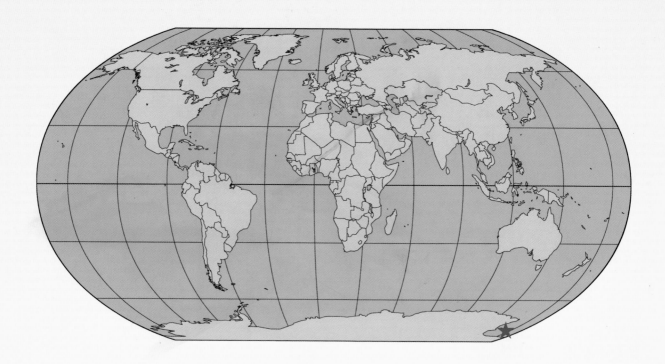

ABOUT THE EMPEROR PENGUIN

Emperor penguins are the largest of the 17 kinds of penguins, and they spend their entire lives in the cold Antarctic.

A female emperor penguin lays one egg and then leaves to feed, traveling across the frozen ice. While the mother is gone, the father keeps the egg on his feet! He stands with the egg balanced on his feet, keeping it warm with a layer of feathered skin, for nearly 65 days! He does not eat anything while he holds the egg.

When the mother returns after two months, the father takes his turn at sea fishing, and the mother cares for her chick.

Did you know that even though penguins are a type of bird, they can't fly?

PICTORIAL GLOSSARY

▲ Wilson's Storm Petrel

▲ Crocodile Fish

▲ South Polar Skua

▲ Leopard Seal

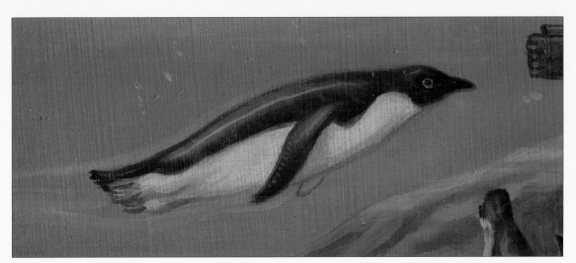

▲ Adelie Penguin

▲ Patagonian Toothfish

▲ **Rookery**

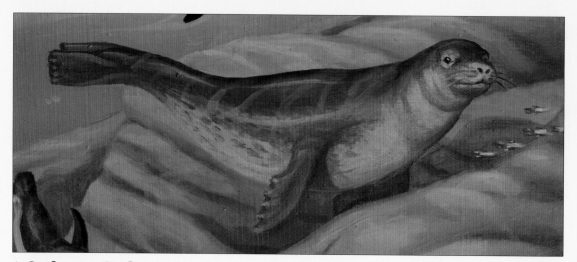

▲ **Crabeater Seal**

▲ **Pleuragramma**

▲ Emperor Penguin

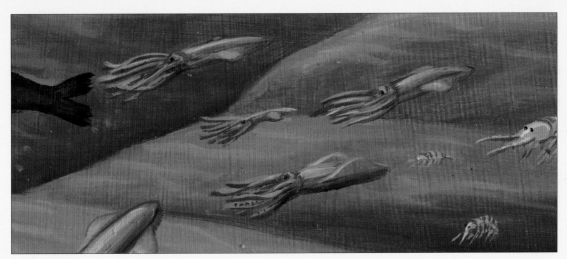

▲ Squid

▲ Krill